CAPTAIN GREEN
AND THE PLASTIC SCENE

Written by EVELYN BOOKLESS   Illustrated by DANNY DEEPTOWN

Marshall Cavendish
Children

For Jack who loved to read, and my heroes, Steve and Cillian

~ E.B.

For River, I hope the animals on the earth today get to grow old with you

~ D.D.

"Hooray!" said Captain Green.

"It's time to practise my superhero skills."

He swooped and
he soared and then
he declared...

"It is I, Captain Green, the Caped Captain of Clean, protecting planet Earth from pollution and grime."

He aimed his green beam at litter and foul-smelling fumes.

ZAP! BAM! POW!

But while flying and flipping, diving and dipping, he crashed. *SLAM!* "Oh, green gravy!"

Just then, his watch glowed. "Someone is calling!" He set off in a flash, but...

…he froze in mid-air
when he saw what it was.

Dolphin was all tangled up.

"Do not fear, the Captain is here!"
Captain Green spun like a whirlwind,
going faster and faster. *WHOOSH!*

Then he snatched the junk
and zoomed straight up,
unravelling Dolphin as he flew.

"Phew. Thank you!" said Dolphin.
"I couldn't escape. There's plastic everywhere."
Dolphin was safe but still looked sad.

Whale, Seal and Fish said they had been hurt too.
"I'll get to the bottom of this," Captain Green
promised, but he wasn't sure how.

As he flew, he wondered where the plastic had come from. Suddenly, his watch glowed again.

Seagull was spluttering and gasping for air.

"Do not fear, the Captain is here!" Using his super-strength, Captain Green lunged towards the bird, grabbed him by the waist and squeezed his belly. *OOMPF!* Out spewed some plastic.

"You saved me. Thank you!" said Seagull.
"I thought I was eating food."
Seagull was better but still looked worried.

"I'll take care of this,"
promised Captain Green.

"What a relief. Thank you!" said Turtle. "I couldn't get back to the sea."
Turtle was free but still looked troubled.

Captain Green's heart sank. "The beach is a MESS!"

He flew off, determined to help his friends.

"Mission complete!"
But then…

"It keeps coming!" said Turtle.
Captain Green gasped. "My green-ness!
I know what's causing this."

He closed his eyes and thought back to Superhero School.

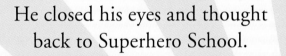

YES!

He knew *just* what to do.

Captain Green shone his signal.
The people gazed up.

"I am Captain Green,

the Caped Captain of Clean,"

he boomed.

"Everyone, STOP! The oceans are

being ruined by all this plastic.

The animals are in danger.

We need to work together!"

Then he shared his plan for all to see.

REDUCE

"Use less! We don't need all this plastic."

"Sounds good to me," said Dolphin.

REUSE

"Use things again." Captain Green showed some children how to make spaceships from empty bottles and bits.

"They look great!" chirped Seagull.

RECYCLE

"If you can't reduce or reuse, put waste in the recycling place.
Then *used* things can be changed into *new* things."

"Green-tastic!" said Turtle.

SHAZAM!

"Thank you everybody," said the animals.
"Let's keep our oceans clear and clean,
and use the three Rs to be green."

Captain Green zoomed up high.
"I'm Captain Green,
the Caped Captain of Clean."

Everyone cheered,
"REDUCE! REUSE! RECYCLE!"

"Remember now,
you don't need superpowers
to save the seas.
It just takes a
super *human*.

KEEP IT GREEN!"

Published by Marshall Cavendish Children
An imprint of Marshall Cavendish International

A member of the
Times Publishing Group

Other Marshall Cavendish Offices:
Marshall Cavendish Corporation. 99 White Plains Road, Tarrytown NY 10591-9001, USA
• Marshall Cavendish International (Thailand) Co Ltd. 253 Asoke, 12th Flr, Sukhumvit 21
Road, Klongtoey Nua, Wattana, Bangkok 10110, Thailand • Marshall Cavendish (Malaysia)
Sdn Bhd, Times Subang, Lot 46, Subang Hi-Tech Industrial Park, Batu Tiga, 40000 Shah
Alam, Selangor Darul Ehsan, Malaysia

Marshall Cavendish is a registered trademark of Times Publishing Limited

National Library Board, Singapore Cataloguing-in-Publication Data

Name(s): Evelyn Bookless. | Deeptown, Danny, illustrator.
Title: Captain Green and the plastic scene / written by Evelyn Bookless ; illustrated by
Danny Deeptown.
Description: Singapore : Marshall Cavendish Children, 2018
Identifier(s): OCN 1026403175 | ISBN 978-981-47-9477-0
Subject(s): LCSH: Plastic scrap--Juvenile fiction. | Recycling (Waste, etc.)--Juvenile fiction
Classification: DDC 428.6--dc23

Printed in Singapore